For Peggy Hageman

First published in Great Britain 2022 by Farshore
An imprint of HarperCollins*Publishers*
1 London Bridge Street, London SE1 9GF
www.farshore.co.uk

HarperCollins*Publishers*
1st Floor, Watermarque Building,
Ringsend Road, Dublin 4, Ireland

First published in the United States of America
by Dial Books for Young Readers,
an imprint of Penguin Random House LLC, 2021

Text and illustrations copyright © Michael Slack 2021
Michael Slack has asserted
his moral rights.

ISBN 978 0 0085 0557 8
Printed in UK
001

A CIP catalogue record for this title is available from the British Library.

Stay safe online. Any website addresses listed in this book are correct at the time of going to print. However, Farshore is
not responsible for content hosted by third parties. Please be aware that online content can be subject to change and
websites can contain content that is unsuitable for children. We advise that all children are supervised when using the internet.

This book was printed in the UK by a CarbonNeutral® company using vegetable-based inks.

MIX
Paper from
responsible sources
FSC
www.fsc.org
FSC C007454

FSC ™ is a non-profit international organisation established to promote
the responsible management of the world's forests. Products carrying the
FSC label are independently certified to assure consumers that they come
from forests that are managed to meet the social, economic and
ecological needs of present and future generations,
and other controlled sources.

Find out more about HarperCollins and the environment at
www.harpercollins.co.uk/green

DINOSAURS ON KITTEN ISLAND

MICHAEL SLACK

Farshore

Dinosaurs, you're bored? That's impossible! You live on Dinosaur Island.

You can . . .

Make a sandcastle. ☑

Watch stuff sink in the tar pit. ☑

Reassemble a skeleton. ☑

What could be more fun than playing on Dinosaur Island?

Playing with the kittens on Kitten Island?

Dinos, that's **bonkers.**

Sure, they look cute and friendly . . .
but really they are fearless and feisty.
Fun with those felines will end in catastrophe.

You do **not want** to play with those kittens.

Too late. You are going to play with the kittens.

Maybe they are taking a cat nap.
You should just let them sleep and head home.

Oh, no! They are wide awake and ready to play.

Dinosaurs, step away from the kittens and go back
to Dinosaur Island where it's safe.

Or . . . don't listen to me and play with these wild cats.

GAME 1:
Launch the Lizards

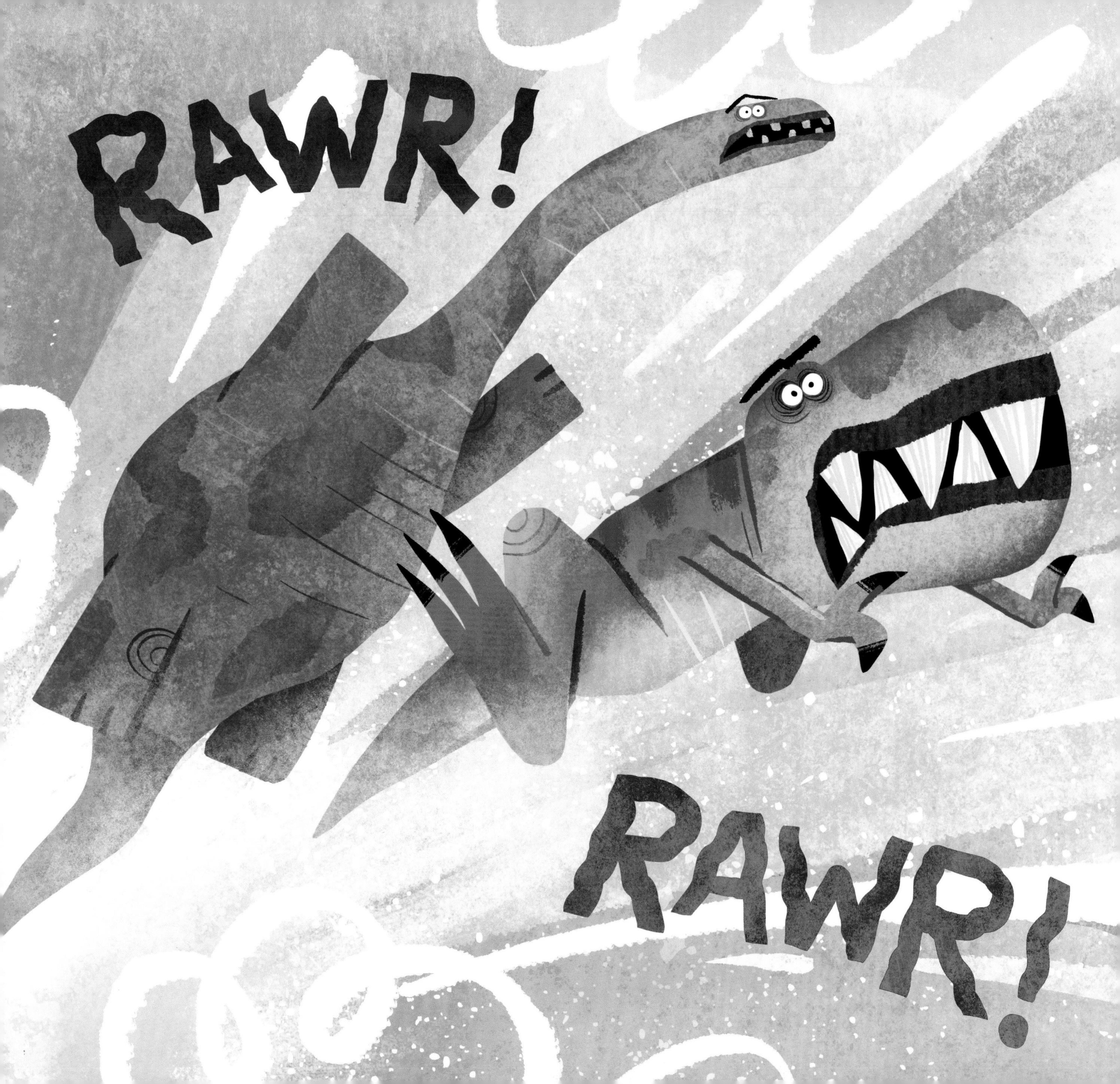
RAWR!
RAWR!

Well, soggysaurs, you're soaked but you survived.
A boring sandcastle sure sounds pretty great right now . . . doesn't it?

Dinosaurs?

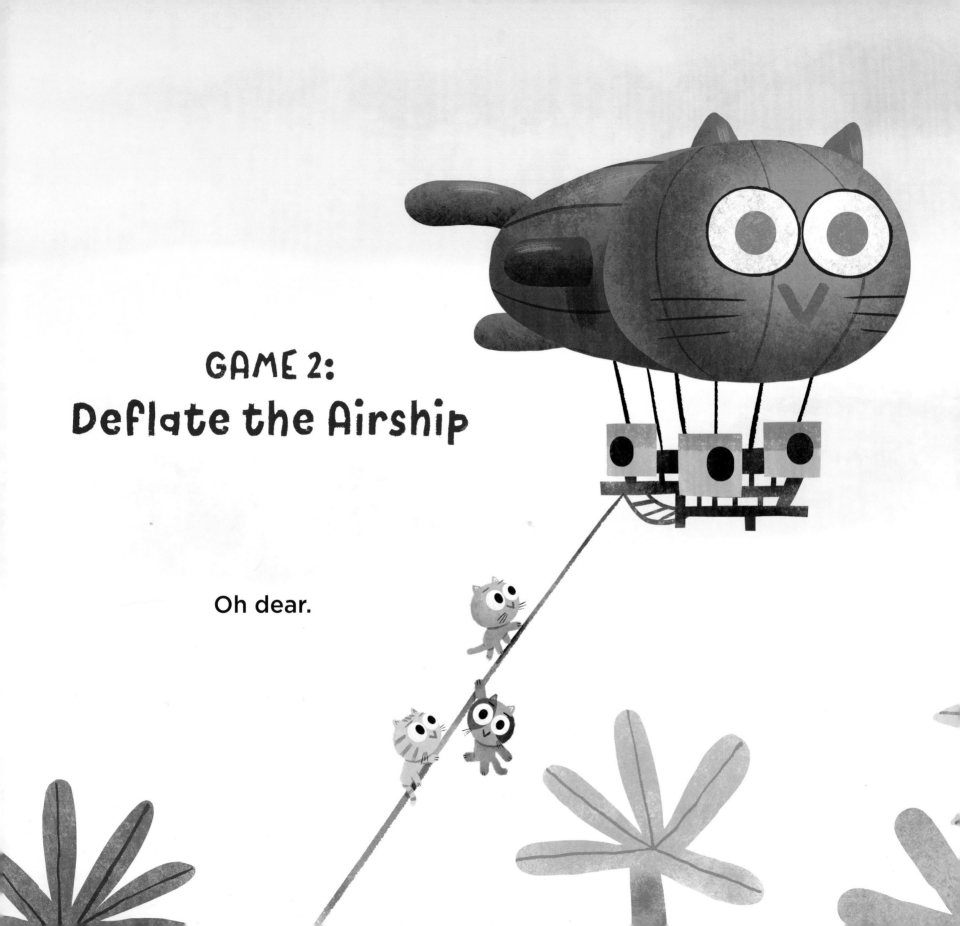

GAME 2:
Deflate the Airship

Oh dear.

Pfffftttttt

This does not look like fun, dinosaurs.

You should leave before you end up as fossils.

Hold on. What are the kittens doing?

This is just embarrassing and super gross.
I have a sinking feeling this is going to end in disaster.

Dinosaurs! I know you want to be friends with these kittens.
But if you don't end this perilous playdate,
you might become **extinct!**

Even fearless furballs know when their friends are not having fun.

I was wrong. You **can** have fun with the kittens on Kitten Island. As long as everyone plays in the Tiny Baby Kitten Playroom.

Where everything is puffy, adorable, and **totally** safe.

Or not.

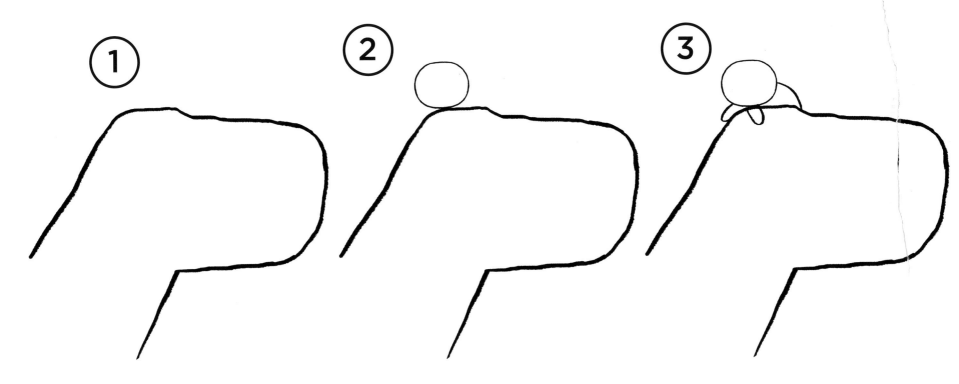

How to draw a

KITTEN ON A DINOSAUR

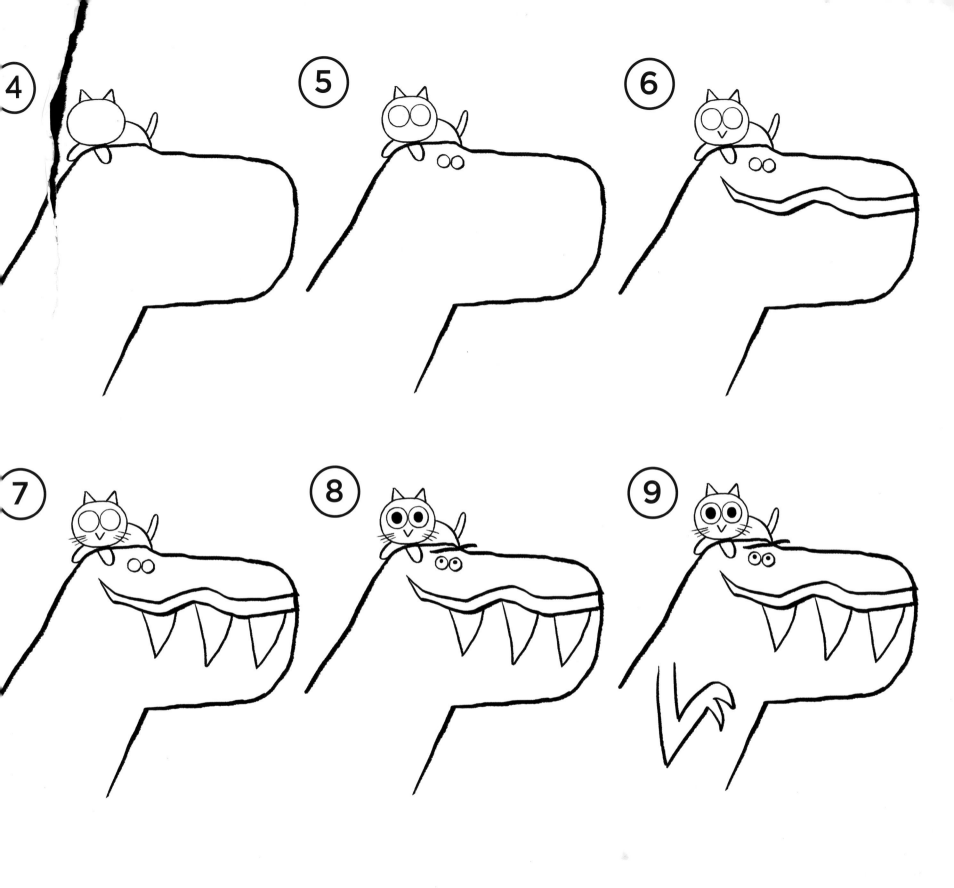

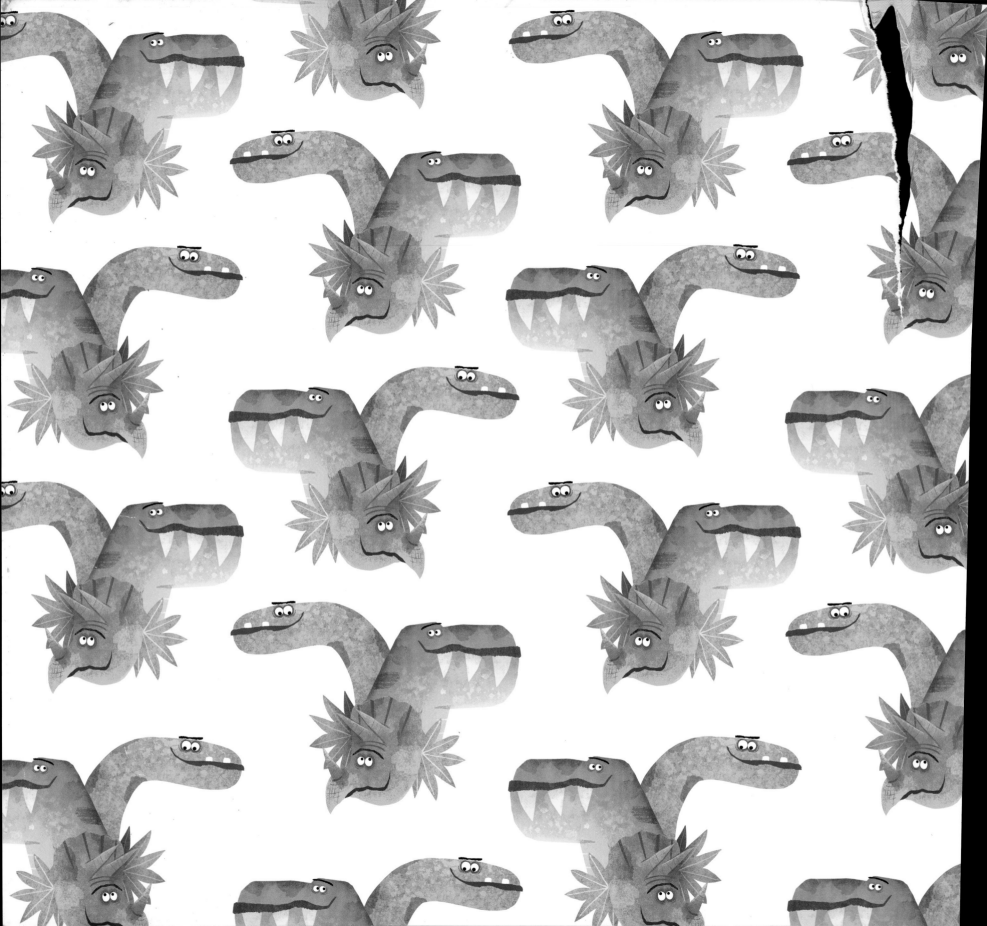